KT-143-799

This book belongs to

....

This edition published by Parragon Books Ltd in 2017

Parragon Books Ltd
Chartist House
15–17 Trim Street
Bath BA1 1HA, UK
www.parragon.com

Copyright © Parragon Books Ltd 2012-2017

Illustrated by: Gail Yerrill
Reading consultant: Geraldine Taylor

All rights reserved. No part of this publication may be reproduced, stored in a retrieval
system or transmitted, in any form or by any means, electronic, mechanical, photocopying,
recording or otherwise, without the prior permission of the copyright holder.

ISBN 978-1-4748-9518-7

Printed in China

My First Storytime
The Elves
and the
Shoemaker

PaRragon

Bath • New York • Cologne • Melbourne • Delhi
Hong Kong • Shenzhen • Singapore

Five steps for enjoyable reading

Traditional stories and fairy tales are a great way to begin reading practice. The stories and characters are familiar and lively. Follow the steps below to help your child become a confident and independent reader:

Step 1
Read the story aloud to your child. Run your finger under the words as you read.

There was once a poor shoemaker and his wife.

"This is my last piece of leather," said the shoemaker, sadly. "I can only make one more pair of shoes."

The shoemaker cut out the leather and put it on his workbench.

8

Step 2
Look at the pictures and talk about what is happening.

Step 3

Read the simple text on the right-hand page together. When reading, some words come up again and again, such as **the, to, and**. Your child will quickly get to recognize these high-frequency words by sight.

They went up to bed.

9

Step 4

When your child is ready, encourage them to read the simple lines on their own.

Step 5

Help your child to complete the puzzles at the back of the book.

There was once a poor shoemaker
and his wife.

"This is my last piece of leather,"
said the shoemaker, sadly. "I can
only make one more pair of shoes."

The shoemaker cut out the leather
and put it on his workbench.

They went up to bed.

The next morning, the old shoemaker found a new pair of shoes on his workbench.

"Who made these shoes?" asked the shoemaker.

He put them in the shop window. A man saw the shoes. He came into the shop and tried them on.

"I like these shoes," said the man.
"I will buy them from you."

Now the
old shoemaker
could buy more
leather. He cut out the
leather and put it on the
workbench. Then he went up
to bed. The next morning, there
was a new pair of boots and a new
pair of shoes on the workbench.

"Who has made these boots and shoes?" asked the shoemaker's wife.

The old shoemaker soon sold both pairs of shoes. Now he could buy even more leather!

He cut out the leather and went up to bed. The next morning, he found eight new pairs of boots and shoes. And so it went on, for weeks and weeks.

Everyone liked his boots and shoes!

Soon they were rich.
But they still didn't know
who was making the shoes.
So they made a plan.

The old shoemaker cut out
the leather. And he put it on
his workbench. But this time they
didn't go to bed. They hid instead.

"Now we will see who makes the shoes," said the shoemaker.

The old shoemaker and his wife
waited and waited. At last, the shop
door opened and two tiny elves ran in.
They jumped up onto the workbench
and sewed the leather as fast as they
could! Like magic, the shoes were
finished. The elves danced a little jig
on the workbench – tip-tip-tap!
Then they jumped down.

The elves ran away into the night.

"Those elves are very kind to us," said the shoemaker.

"Yes," said his wife. "But their clothes are old and thin. They must be so cold."

The shoemaker nodded his head.

"The winter snow is on the ground and they don't even have any shoes," he said.

"How can we help the elves?"
said the shoemaker's wife.

The next day, the shoemaker and his wife set to work.

What do you think they made? That's right: two tiny coats, two tiny pairs of trousers and two tiny pairs of boots.

They looked just right for the tiny elves.

They put the presents on the workbench. Then they waited and waited. At last, the shop door opened and in ran the two tiny elves. They jumped up onto the workbench and saw the presents. They danced a little jig.

Tip-tip-tap!
"Two for you and two for me!"

The tiny elves put on the tiny clothes.

"They are just right!" they said.

They danced a little jig all along the workbench – tip-tip-tap!

"Thank you," they called as they jumped down.

The tiny elves did another jig on their way out of the shop – tip-tip-tap!

Puzzle time!

Which two words rhyme?

for   can   run   man   his

Which word does not match the picture?

elves

jig

night

Which word matches the picture?

shop

shoe

show

Who cuts the leather?

shoemaker

wife

elves

Which sentence is right?

They sewed as fast as they could.

They sewed as slowly as they could.

Puzzle time! Answers
Which two words rhyme? for (can) run (man) his
Which word does not match the picture? elves jig (night)
Which word matches the picture? (shoe) shop show
Who cuts the leather? (shoemaker) wife elves
Which sentence is right? (They sewed as fast as they could.) They sewed as slowly as they could.

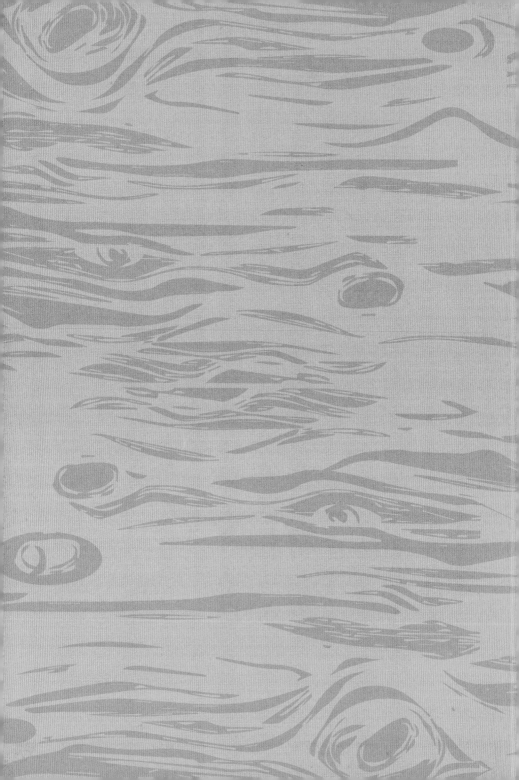